First published in Great Britain in 1993
by Simon & Schuster Young Books
Campus 400
Maylands Avenue
Hemel Hempstead
Herts HP2 7EZ

Reprinted in 1993
Text © 1993 Robert Swindells
Illustrations © 1993 Val Biro

Typeset in 16/24pt Times Educational by Goodfellow & Egan Ltd,
Cambridge
Printed and bound in Portugal by Ediçoes ASA

British Library Cataloguing in Publication Data available

ISBN 0 7500 1335 4
ISBN 0 7500 1336 2 (pbk)

Robert Swindells

Sam and Sue and Lavatory Lou

(Barney's in there somewhere too!)

Illustrated by Val Biro

SIMON & SCHUSTER
YOUNG BOOKS

CHAPTER ONE

Sam and Sue were walking through the park. They were on their way to the funfair with three pounds they'd saved up. They'd just passed the pond when Sam said, "I have to spend a penny."

Sue laughed. "A penny? What can you get for a penny? The cheapest ride's twenty pence."

"I don't mean that," said Sam. "I mean – you know."

"Oh – oh right. Yes. Off you go then. I'll wait here."

Sue leaned against a tree, listening to the funfair music. Sam vanished into the Gents.

Two and a half seconds later, he was back with a funny look on his face.

"That was quick," said Sue.

"I haven't been yet," Sam told her. "There's a man in there."

"So what?"

"There's something funny about him. Come and have a look."

"I can't go in the Gents, dummy!"

"You're scared, that's why."

"No I'm not."

"Have a look, then."

"Oh, all right." Sue glanced around to make sure nobody was watching. She was a bit scared, but she wasn't going to let Sam see.

It was a bit dim in the Gents,
but there was enough light for
Sue to see that Sam was right.
There he was, in the corner
by the washbasin. Except that
he wasn't a man at all.
He was a ghost.

Sue didn't hang about.

9

"That was even quicker," said Sam
sarcastically.

"It's not a man," Sue whispered. "It's a
ghost."

"How d'you know?"

"Men aren't white all over and they don't
come to a point at the bottom."

"Right. So what do we do?"

"Go to the fair," said Sue.

"But what about him?"

"What about him?"

"We can't just leave him in there. He'll scare people. And anyway, I still haven't spent that penny."

"Can't you wait till afterwards?"

"No."

"So what d'you think we should do?"

"Ask him to leave."

Sue laughed nervously. "Have you ever tried asking a ghost to leave?"

"'Course not. I've never ridden the Flying Carpet either, but I will today. There's a first time for everything."

"Okay," said Sue. "But you go first. It *is* the Gents, after all."

So they marched inside, Sam leading. The ghost was sitting on the rim of the washbasin with its head bowed and its hands over its face. It looked so fed up that the twins forgot to be scared.

"Uh – hello," said Sue. "I'm Sue and he's Sam."

The ghost uncovered its face and nodded at them.

"How do you do. I'm supposed to be haunting this place, scaring people to death, but it isn't working. I mean, you came back, and you're only about eight years old."

"I'm nine," said Sue.

"Is that why you're looking so sad?" asked Sam. "Because you can't frighten people?"

"Oh, I can frighten people all right." The ghost sounded indignant. "I've had them leaping out of upstairs windows in nothing but their knickers, but not here – not in a place like this."

He looked at the twins. "Have you ever heard of a haunted lavatory? Is there a video called 'The Lavatory Ghost'? Of course there isn't. It sounds ridiculous, and it is."

"Then why are you here?" asked Sue.
"Did you die here or something?"

"No, of course I didn't. I'm here because
everyone's got to be somewhere, and
they've flattened my haunt."

"Your haunt?" said Sam. "What's that?"

"A haunt's a place where there's a ghost.
You know that derelict house on the
corner of Spencer Road?"

"Oooh yes!" shivered Sam. "We call it
the haunted house."

"Yes, and so it was, young man, because
I haunted it; but they've bulldozed it.
Smashed it to bits and carted the bits away
in trucks. There's just a flattened garden
now, so I wandered about until I found this
place."

"But why don't you find a house to haunt?" asked Sue. "There are plenty of them about."

The ghost sighed. "It's not as easy as that. The old houses have their own ghosts and the modern ones aren't suitable. You can't haunt them. You wear yourself out clanking and moaning and they say 'Oh, it's the central heating or the floorboards settling.' There are no dark corners with cobwebs and rats and spiders, you see."

"So you're stuck here?" said Sam.

The ghost nodded glumly. "Looks like it, unless you've got a better idea."

"Not at the moment," said Sue. "But if we think of anything we'll let you know. Have you got a name, by the way?"

The ghost pulled a face. "Oh, I've got a name all right, but I was hoping you wouldn't ask. It's Lou."

"Lou!" Sam laughed out loud. "That's a wicked name for someone who lives in a lavatory."

"I know," groaned Lou. "That's what all my friends say. They call me Lavatory Lou. It stops being funny after a while."

"It's funny to me," chuckled Sam.

"Yes, well," growled Lou. "It's not your problem, is it?"

"Listen," said Sam. "Sue and I will keep our eyes skinned for a really creepy old house, right? And in the meantime, would you mind stepping outside for a minute? I need this place to myself."

"Of course." Lou bowed like a
gentleman in a very old movie.

"I shall hope to see you later, then.
Come along, Sue."

CHAPTER TWO

"Poor old Lou," said Sam a few minutes later, as the twins walked up the grassy slope to the funfair. "We really should try to find a place for him, Sue."

"We will," Sue promised. "And in the meantime we've got to decide what to go on first."

They tried the Flying Carpet, which churned up their lunches quite a lot. Then they went on something called Tarantula which whirled them and spun them at a terrific speed in all directions, including upside down.

When they got off, Sam could hardly walk and Sue wasn't exactly dying for a hot-dog either. "You could be sick down the back of your own neck on that thing," she moaned.

They walked about, watching people enjoy themselves. It was a warm, sunny afternoon and the funfair was crowded.

Presently Sam said, "Hey look, Sue – a ghost train."

"Where?"

"Over there – Barney's Ghost Train, it says. Fancy a go on that?"

"Not particularly, Sam. I mean, we've seen a real ghost, haven't we? We're not going to be scared by pretend ones. And anyway, hardly anybody's going on it."

This was true. The train had ten cars, and seven were empty. A sad-looking man with white whiskers and an engine driver's cap was standing by the train, waiting for customers. Sue felt a bit sorry for him.

"Okay Sam," she said. "We'll give it a go."

The twins went over to the man. "Two please," said Sue. "Are you Barney?"

The man nodded. "That's me." He took Sue's money and tore two tickets off a roll. "There y'are. Anywhere you like."

"When does the train go?" asked Sam.
"When it's full?"

Barney shook his head. "Nay, we'd wait forever if we waited for that. People don't seem to want ghost trains any more."

"Why not?"

"Well." Barney nodded towards Tarantula. "That, for a start. There are all these exciting new rides. I guess they make the old ghost train seem pretty tame."

The twins climbed into an empty car. A few more people got on. The train was just about to move when three big boys came out of the crowd and went up to Barney.

"Oh, no!" groaned Sue. "Look who's showed up, Sam."

Sam looked. "Oh crikey – it's the Bazzard gang. Duck down, Sue. Don't let 'em see us."

Gaz Bazzard was the school bully. He was in the top class, and he terrorised the playground with his two mates, Mick and Steve.

Sue ducked, but it was too late. Gaz had spotted her. "Well," he cried. "Look who's riding the ghost train. Sam and Sue, the terrified two. Let's get on behind 'em."

CHAPTER THREE

The bullies clambered aboard and the train set off, clanking and rumbling into a cold black tunnel. Ghosts and skeletons appeared, glowing with a greenish light, and something touched Sue's face, but the bullies only laughed.

"Plastic!" they cried. "Luminous paint. Bits of old cloth."

"I wish they'd shut up," whispered Sue. "They're spoiling the fun."

She'd hardly got the words out when someone grabbed a handful of her hair and jerked her head back. "What did you say?" snarled Gaz.

"N-nothing," gasped Sue.

"Oh yes, you did." Gaz squeezed till her scalp really hurt.

"What did you say, fish-face?"

"Leave her alone!" cried Sam. "She didn't say anything."

"Who rattled your cage, slime-features?" Gaz turned to his mates. "Hey Mick, here's a little runt needs his lugs twisting."

Sam tried to dodge, but Mick seized both his ears and twisted them viciously.

"Ow!" yelled Sam. "You're pulling 'em off, you big dummy!" His eyes were watering.

"Dummy?" Mick twisted harder. "Big dummy?" Another twist. "Is that what you called me, runt?"

"No. Yes. Gerroff, you great lump!"

The ride continued, but the twins got no fun out of it. The three bullies slapped and nudged and pulled them about, laughing and jeering, till the train burst out into sunlight, slowing down.

As soon as it stopped, the twins scrambled out of their car. The Bazzard gang stayed in theirs, looking sweet and innocent. They were off round again to spoil somebody else's fun.

"Hey, what's the matter?" Barney had noticed that the twins looked upset. "Did my ghost train scare you that much?"

Sam shook his head. "No."

"Then what is it?"

"It's nothing, Barney," said Sue. "Honestly. We'll be all right in a minute." She forced a smile for the kindly showman, but she didn't feel like smiling.

CHAPTER FOUR

The twins left the funfair and walked down the grassy slope. "That Barney," said Sue, when she felt a bit better. "He's nice, isn't he? I wish more people would go on his ghost train."

"It needs livening up a bit," said Sam. "Gaz was right, Sue, even though he is a bully. You can tell everything's made of paint and plastic and bits of cloth. What Barney needs is—"

"A real ghost!" cried Sue. "That's what you were going to say, weren't you?"

Sam nodded, grinning. "And we know where there is one, don't we? C'mon Sue – time to spend another penny."

They found Lou practising his groan in the Gents.

"Hey, Lou!" cried Sam. "How'd you like to get out of here?"

Lou gazed at him sadly. "I hate this place, Sam, but if I leave I'll have nowhere to go at all."

"Yes you will!" cried Sue. "Listen.

How'd you fancy a dark,
cold place full of cobwebs
and spiders and lots of
other scary stuff, with
trainloads of nervous
people coming through
every few minutes?"

Lou sighed. "That would
be heaven, Sue. Pure heaven,
but there's no such place."

"Yes there is!" whooped Sam.
"Come with us."

As they led him towards the funfair, Sue and Sam told Lou about Barney, and how the ghost-train was failing, and what the Bazzard gang had done to them.

When they'd finished, Lou said: "Listen. I'm going to make Barney's ghost train the scariest ride in the funfair, and I think I could fix Bazzard and his friends as well if they happened to be around."

"They *are* around – look!" Sue pointed.
The train had emerged from the tunnel and
was stopping. Gaz and his mates were in
the same car they'd occupied before.

As the train stopped, a small boy got
out of the car the twins had ridden in.
He was in tears.

"They've been up to their tricks again,"
said Sam.

The small boy ran away, and everybody else got off the train. The Bazzard gang started to get off too.

"Quick!" hissed Lou. "Get on board while I slip into the tunnel. They'll go round again if they've got you to torment. And don't be surprised by anything you see!"

CHAPTER FIVE

Gaz Bazzard could hardly believe his luck when Sam and Sue appeared. "Well," he purred. "If it isn't the terrified twins again, and they haven't brought Mummy either. I reckon we'll go round one more time, eh, lads?"

The train began to move. As soon as they were inside, the bullies started laughing and whistling and shouting scornful comments. When something white swooped down, Gaz yelled, "Look out – somebody's washing blew away!"

But when it passed very close to them and a hollow voice moaned, "*Beware the Train of Hazard, Bazzard*," their laughter dried up.

"Here," said Gaz, scowling at his companions in the dark. "Which one of you said that?"

"I didn't," said Mick.

"Me neither," said Steve.

Sue and Sam giggled.

The train swung round a bend and a great vampire bat came flapping out of the dark. There were screams from some of the passengers as the creature wafted overhead. It skimmed twittering over Gaz's car and the three lads had to duck.

An icy draught fanned them, and when they raised their heads they were speeding towards a gigantic, luminous skull which waited with gaping jaws to swallow the train.

Squeals and gasps came from the riders, but at the last second the skull vanished, to be replaced by a great glowing spider which galloped along beside the train, close to where the Bazzard gang was sitting.

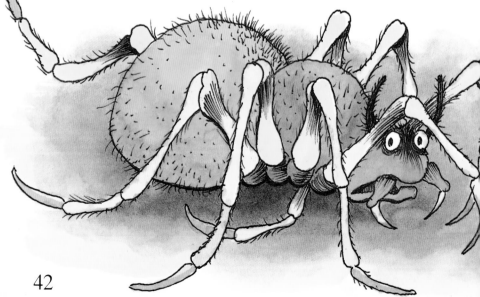

Gaz let out a yelp and buried his head in Steve's lap. When the spider became a slavering werewolf, he burst into tears.

After that there was an ogre, a witch and a giant toad roaring fire. All of these creatures seemed to be after Gaz and his mates, and long before the ride was over the Bazzard gang was in a blubbering huddle on the floor.

The instant the train left the tunnel they
leapt from the car in a tangle of arms and
legs, and ran.

The passengers were getting off the train,
waving their arms and chattering excitedly.
One of them called out, "Great ride,
Barney – best I've ever had!" Some
weren't getting off – they wanted to go
round again.

44

Barney collected fares as new passengers came hurrying to try this fantastic ride everybody was talking about.

Sam and Sue went off feeling fine. Tomorrow was pocket-money day and they'd be back. Gaz and his mates wouldn't, and they'd be a bit quieter in the playground from now on, too, especially if someone whispered "Ghost train" at them.

Barney was happy, and so were his passengers. Even the sun seemed a little brighter.

And Lavatory Lou? Well, he wasn't
Lavatory Lou any more. Locomotive Lou,
his friends called him now, and that made
him just about the happiest ghost alive. Or
not alive.

Sue and Sam hadn't said goodbye to him,
but that was all right. They'd be seeing a
lot of him from now on, as they rode the
greatest ghost train in the world.

STORYBOOKS

*Look out for these exciting new books in the Storybooks series
by Simon & Schuster Young Books:*

Mandy's Mermaid by Anne Forsyth
Judy and the Martian by Penelope Lively
Matthew and the Sea Singer by Jill Paton Walsh
The Birthday Phone by Toby Forward
TV Genie by John Talbot
The Thing in the Sink by Frieda Hughes
Hopping Mad by Nick Warburton
Babybug by Catherine Storr
Dreamy Daniel, Brainy Bert by Scoular Anderson
Look Out, Loch Ness Monster! by Keith Brumpton
The Magic Birthday by Adele Geras
Seymour Finds a Home by Dyan Sheldon
Wonderwitch by Helen Muir
The Twitches by Roy Apps
Fair's Fair by Leon Garfield
Mr Dunfilling by Rob Lewis

These books can be bought at your local bookshop. If you'd
like to find out more about Storybooks, contact *The Sales
Department, Simon & Schuster Young Books, Campus 400,
Maylands Avenue, Hemel Hempstead, Herts HP2 7EZ.*